MARTHA SPEAKS™

Fireworks for All

MARTHA HABLA:
Fuegos artificiales para todos

Adaptation by Karen Barss
Based on a TV series teleplay written by Dietrich Smith

Adaptado por Karen Barss. Basado en un guión para televisión escrito por Dietrich Smith

Based on the characters created by Susan Meddaugh
Basado en los personajes creados por Susan Meddaugh

HOUGHTON MIFFLIN HARCOURT
Boston • New York • 2011

Ages 5–7 • Grade: 2
Guided Reading Level: J
Reading Recovery Level: 17

Edad: 5 a 7 años • Grado: 2.°
Nivel de lectura guiada: J
Nivel de *"Reading Recovery"*: 17

For information about permission to reproduce selections from this book, write to Permissions, Houghton Mifflin Harcourt Publishing Company, 215 Park Avenue South, New York, New York 10003.

Library of Congress Cataloging-in-Publication Data is on file.

ISBN 978-0-547-42892-5 pb | ISBN 978-0-547-42897-0 hc | ISBN 978-0-547-55620-8 bilingual

Design by Rachel Newborn

www.hmhbooks.com
www.marthathetalkingdog.com

Manufactured in Singapore / TWP 10 9 8 7 6 5 4 3 2 1
4500275960

Hooray! ¡Hurra!

School is out for the summer!
¡Comienzan las vacaciones de verano!

"What do you love most about summer?" asks Helen.
"No school!" says T.D.
"No school, and ice cream!" says Alice.

—¿Qué es lo que más les gusta del verano? —pregunta Helena.
—¡Que no hay clases! —dice Toni.
—¡Que no hay clases y que comemos helado! —dice Alicia.

"And every Saturday night," says Helen, ". . . *fireworks!*"

—Y todos los sábados por la noche —dice Helena—,
... *¡fuegos artificiales!*

"They start next Saturday," Truman says.
Martha begins to worry.

—Comienzan el próximo sábado —dice Truman.
Martha empieza a preocuparse.

"I think fireworks are kind of scary," Martha says.
"Scary? No way!" Helen replies.

—Creo que los fuegos artificiales asustan —dice Martha.
—¿Asustan? ¡No, para nada!
—contesta Helena.

Later, Helen's family eats dinner. Mom asks, "Did you hear that Mrs. Demson wants to ban fireworks? Her goal is to have many people sign the ban."

Más tarde, la familia de Helena cena. Mamá les pregunta: —¿Sabían que la señora Demson quiere prohibir los fuegos artificiales? Su meta es lograr que muchas personas firmen la prohibición.

"If you ban fireworks, do you stop them?" asks Martha. "Yes," says Helen. "That would be too bad."

—Si prohíben los fuegos artificiales, ¿los pararán? —pregunta Martha. —Así es —dice Helena—. Sería una lástima.

Martha meets her friends.
They are all very sad.
Fireworks are scary to dogs.

Martha se reúne con sus amigos.
Todos están muy tristes.
Los fuegos artificiales asustan a los perros.

Ruff, woof, growl!
"Fireworks are too loud," Martha agrees.
"But there is something we can do to stop them."

¡Guau, arf, grrr!
—Los fuegos artificiales hacen mucho ruido —dice
Martha—. Pero podemos hacer algo para pararlos.

The dogs go to the park.
"We want to help ban fireworks," Martha tells
Mrs. Demson.

Los perros van al parque.
—Queremos ayudar a prohibir los fuegos artificiales
—le dice Martha a la señora Demson.

But Mrs. Demson does not like dogs.
"Go away! Shoo!" she says.

Pero a la señora Demson no le gustan los perros.
—¡Fuera de aquí! ¡Largo! —les dice.

"I have another plan," Martha tells her friends.
"I can talk. I will ask people to sign the ban."

—Tengo otro plan —les dice Martha a sus amigos—.
Yo puedo hablar. Le pediré a la gente que firme
la prohibición.

At the park, people sign their names.
Mrs. Demson is happy. So is Martha.

En el parque, la gente firma con su nombre.
La señora Demson está feliz. ¡Y Martha también!

"That's it," says Mrs. Demson at the end of the day.
"No more fireworks!"

—Hemos terminado —dice la señora Demson al final
del día—. ¡No habrá más fuegos artificiales!

"No more fireworks?" says Helen.
She rushes to tell her friends.

—¿No habrá más fuegos artificiales? —dice Helena.
Corre a contárselo a sus amigos.

Martha meets the gang.
"Hi," she says. "What's up?"
"Nothing," T.D. says. "Summer is ruined, that's all."

Martha se reúne con la pandilla.
—Hola —les dice—. ¿Qué pasa?
—Nada —dice Toni—. Se arruinó el verano, eso es todo.

Martha looks at the poster.
"I am sorry, but fireworks are really scary for dogs."

Martha mira el cartel.
—Lo siento, pero los fuegos artificiales asustan mucho a
los perros.

Helen asks, "Scary? Really?"
"I tried to tell you," says Martha.
"They are too loud."

—¿Se asustan? —pregunta Helena—. ¿En serio?
—Traté de decírtelo —responde Martha—. Hacen mucho ruido.

"Martha, I'm so sorry I did not listen," Helen says. "I have an idea that can save the fireworks *and* your ears."

—Martha, lamento mucho no haberte escuchado —dice Helena—. Tengo una idea que puede salvar los fuegos artificiales y tus oídos.

"You can watch *Courageous Collie Carlo* shows at the movie theater," says Helen. "You won't hear the fireworks."

—Pueden ir al cine a ver las películas de Carlo, el collie valiente —dice Helena—. Así no oirán los fuegos artificiales.

"A special evening show just for dogs!"
says Martha. "Every dog in town will be there!"

¡Será un evento especial sólo para perros!
—dice Martha—. ¡Todos los perros de la ciudad
irán a verlo!